This book is
your passport
into time.

Can you survive
in the
Civil War era?
Turn the page
to find out.

Bantam Books in the Time Machine Series
Ask your bookseller for the books you have missed

TIME MACHINE 5

Civil War
Secret Agent

by Steve Perry
illustrated by Alex Nino

A Byron Preiss Book

BANTAM BOOKS
TORONTO · NEW YORK · LONDON · SYDNEY · AUCKLAND

To Slick

RL 4, IL age 10 and up

CIVIL WAR SECRET AGENT
A Bantam Book/December 1984

Special thanks to Ann Hodgman, Ron Buehl, Anne Greenberg,
Debbie Trentalange, Pauline Bigornia and Ruth Ashby.

Book design by Alex Jay
Cover painting by Steve Fastner
Cover design by Alex Jay
Mechanicals by Studio J
Typesetting by Graphic/Data Services

Associate editors: Ann Weil and Jim Gasperini

"Time Machine" is a trademark of
Byron Preiss Visual Publications, Inc.

ATTENTION TIME TRAVELER!

This book is your time machine. Do not read it through from beginning to end. In a moment you will receive a mission, a special task that will take you to another time period. As you face the dangers of history, the Time Machine often will give you options of where to go or what to do.

This book also contains a Data Bank to tell you about the age you are going to visit. You can use this Data Bank to help you make your choices. Or you can take your chances without reading it. It is up to you to decide.

In the back of this book is a Data File. It contains hints to help you if you are not sure what choice to make. The following symbol appears next to any choices for which there is a hint in the Data File.

To complete your mission as quickly as possible, you may wish to use the Data Bank and the Data File together.

There is one correct end to this Time Machine mission. You must reach it or risk being stranded in time!

THE FOUR RULES OF TIME TRAVEL

As you begin your mission, you must observe the following rules. Time Travelers who do not follow these rules risk being stranded in time.

1. You must not kill any person or animal.

2. You must not try to change history. Do not leave anything from the future in the past.

3. You must not take anybody when you jump in time. Avoid disappearing in a way that scares people or makes them suspicious.

4. You must follow instructions given to you by the Time Machine. You must choose from the options given to you by the Time Machine.

YOUR MISSION

Your mission is to travel back to America in the days before the Civil War and find Harriet Tubman, the leader of the Underground Railroad, which was a network of people who helped slaves escape to freedom in the North.

In 1859, a black man named Thomas Dean disappeared from the Jasper plantation in Maryland. A diary, recently discovered in an attic in Philadelphia, says that Thomas Dean, who was a slave, managed to escape from the cruel owners of the plantation with the help of Harriet Tubman.

Harriet herself was a slave and escaped to Philadelphia in 1849. She was one of the bravest freedom fighters of the Civil War era, and the hero of many tales of that time.

Did Harriet Tubman really help Thomas Dean? Or did he disappear in some other mysterious way?

You must find Harriet Tubman and solve the mystery of Thomas Dean.

 To activate the Time Machine, turn the page.

**TIME TRAVEL ACTIVATED.
Stand by for Equipment.**

EQUIPMENT

You are allowed to take four items with you on your trip back into the past. Choose which four items you want from the list below.

A ball of string.
A small flashlight. ✓
A pocketknife. ✓
A box of matches. ✓
Ten dollars in Union money.
Ten dollars in Confederate money. √
A firecracker.
A pocket watch.

To begin your mission now, turn to page 1.

To learn more about the time to which you will be traveling, go on to the next page.

DATA BANK

TIMELINE

1820-21	Harriet Tubman was born.
1844	Harriet married John Tubman.
1849	Harriet escaped to Philadelphia and freedom.
1850-61	Harriet was a "conductor" on the Underground Railroad.
April 1859	The Nalle Incident.
April 1861	The Civil War started.
November 1861	The Battle of Hilton Head.
March 1862	The Battle of the Ironclads.
July 1863	The Battle of Gettysburg.
November 1863	The Gettysburg Address.
April 1865	Lee surrenders to Grant, effectively ending the Civil War.

Abraham Lincoln is assassinated. |

1) The Civil War between the "free" states and the "slave" states began in 1861 and lasted four years. The Northern "free" states were called the Union side, and the Southern "slave" states were called the Confederate side.

2) The turning point of the war was the Battle of Gettysburg, fought July 1-3, 1863, and won by the Union side.

3) The first battle between two iron ships, the *Monitor* and the *Merrimack,* took place on March 9, 1862. The *Monitor* was protecting the Union warship *Minnesota,* which had run aground near the mouth of the James River.

4) The *Merrimack* was captured by the South and renamed *Virginia* in 1861.

5) The North won a major sea and land battle at Port Royal, near Hilton Head Island, South Carolina, in November 1861.

6) Union uniforms were blue.

7) Confederate uniforms were gray.

8) Abraham Lincoln was assassinated in April 1865.

9) The gun that killed President Lincoln was a derringer, made in Philadelphia.

10) Another name for the Big Dipper during the Civil War was "the drinkin' gourd."

11) If you draw a line between the two stars

Eastern States, 1861

New Hampshire
Vermont
Massachusetts
Rhode Island
Maine
New York
Michigan
Wisconsin
Pennsylvania
Mason-Dixon line
Connecticut
New Jersey
Delaware
Maryland
Illinois
Indiana
Ohio
Virginia
Kentucky
Tennessee
North Carolina
South Carolina
Mississippi
Alabama
Georgia
Florida

☐ Union States
▨ Confederate States

farthest from the "handle" of the Big Dipper and point the line toward the top of the "cup," it points to the North Star.

12) Harriet Tubman was born on a plantation in Dorchester County, Maryland. The plantation and slave owner was Edward Brodas.

13) Harriet Tubman had a head injury as a child, which sometimes caused her to fall into a deep trancelike sleep.

14) Harriet married John Tubman in 1844. She escaped to freedom in 1849. After escaping from slavery, Harriet returned nineteen times to help other slaves escape, including her parents, whom she took to Auburn, New York.

15) Harriet's nickname was Moses.

16) Harriet never learned to read or write.

17) Harriet helped slaves until the war began, then worked as a nurse, guide, and spy for the Union side until the war was over. During her days as a "conductor" on the Underground Railroad, Harriet traveled from her home in Philadelphia back into the slave states to help others escape.

18) According to the diary, the Dean family consisted of Thomas, his wife, Lee Ann, and his daughter, Sarah Mae, who were all active in the antislavery movement.

19) Thomas Dean was freed from slavery in 1859 by four people who broke his chains with an ax.

20) People on the Underground Railroad often used pseudonyms, or false names . . . to confuse their enemies.

DATA BANK COMPLETED. TURN THE PAGE TO BEGIN YOUR MISSION.

 Don't forget, when you see this symbol, you can check the Data File in the back of the book for a hint.

You are in Dorchester County, Maryland, in the winter of 1849. It is very cold; your breath makes thick fog in the icy air. You look around and see that you are out in the country. There are a lot of bare trees along the narrow dirt road you're on, and no sign of people or a town.

You start walking. You know that Harriet Tubman escaped from here to freedom in Philadelphia. It will probably be easier to find her now, before she starts moving around on the Underground Railroad.

You see a row of run-down shacks just off the road ahead. You walk to the nearest one and knock. A tall black man opens the door. "Can I help you?" he asks.

"I'm looking for Harriet Tubman," you say.

He looks around behind you nervously. "Come inside."

Inside is a woman sitting on a stool made of an old tree stump; behind her are six or seven small children. The inside of the shack looks terrible: The wood is bare, there are cracks in the wall as big as your fingers, and the windows are covered with old gunny sacks. It is almost as cold inside as it is outside. A small fire in the tiny fireplace is the only heat.

"What for you askin' 'bout Miz Tubman?"

the man says suspiciously.

"It's important that I talk to her," you say.

The man looks at the woman. She nods. He turns back toward you. "She done escaped," he says. "She was livin' with Dr. Thompson, but she's gone."

Too late, you think, you missed her. You look around the inside of the cabin, which is hardly any shelter at all. If this is how slaves live, you don't wonder why Harriet ran away.

Suddenly there's a pounding at the door. "Open up, Zeb!"

The black man next to you sucks in a quick breath. "It's Master Corey Simon!" he says, looking scared. "My master's boy!" Zeb quickly opens the door.

There is a boy of about twelve standing there, holding a bullwhip. He sees you. "Aha!" he says. "I heard there was a stranger nosing around the slave quarters. What business do you have here?"

You decide your mission is none of this loud-mouthed boy's business, so you don't say anything.

Corey Simon waves the whip at Zeb. "All right. You better tell me, Zeb, or I'll give one of your children ten lashes!"

You don't want to get Zeb or his family into trouble. "I'm looking for Harriet Tubman," you say, staring at the boy.

"What are you doing asking about an escaped slave? You must be some kind of troublemaker! Maybe even helping those aboli-

4

tionists! We know how to deal with people like you!" Corey raises the whip to hit you, but before he can swing it, you dive past him and run out the door, knocking him to one side. You get up and start running.

Corey Simon begins yelling, and when you look over your shoulder, you see four or five men running up to him. He points at you. "Get that kid!" he shouts. They all begin to chase you.

You see an old barn just ahead. Quickly you run inside. No help here; all that's inside is sweet-smelling hay. You try to catch your breath, but you hear the men outside.

"I'll look in the barn!" one yells.

"I'll go with you!" That's Corey Simon's voice. "My whip is going to get a workout on that troublemaker!"

Bad news, you decide. Better try to pick up Harriet's trail somewhere else. Maybe Philadelphia would be better. Or you could go back further in time to try and find her here, say six or seven years before she leaves. But you'd better do something fast—the barn door is beginning to open!

 Jump to Philadelphia. Turn to page 10.

 Jump to Dorchester County, 1843. Turn to page 12.

ou don't know these people. "I think maybe I'll just wait for her to get back," you say. Can you trust them?

The man nods. "Up to you. When she comes back, we'll tell her you're looking for her."

You and Sarah Mae turn to leave. Sarah Mae says. "I know a good place to stay—if you got any money."

You reach into your pocket. You were going to bring some money, but you aren't sure if you did.

 If you brought ten dollars in Union money, turn to page 28.

 If you didn't bring Union money, turn to page 24.

Oh-oh. Tied to a tree in Dorchester County in the cold and no knife. This will be tougher than you thought. You start working on the knots with your teeth.

You're so busy with this that you don't notice the sound of hoofbeats until it's too late. Corey Simon is back—and with four friends.

One of the men tosses a rope over a tree branch. There is a hangman's noose on one end. You gulp and count the loops that make up the noose as the rope dangles in the cold air.

The men untie you and sit you on Corey's horse. One of them laughs as he slips the noose around your neck and pulls it tight. You feel the rough rope rub against your skin. "Who'll do the honors?" one of the men asks.

"*I* will," Corey says. He grins at you and walks toward the horse. All he has to do is swat the animal and it will jump, leaving you hanging. Corey raises his hand—

"Somebody's coming!" one of the men says.

Corey turns to look, his hand still above the horse's flank.

You look. Three men on horses are riding up. One of them has a rifle. The man with the rifle says, "Hold up, there, boys. What's going on?"

"We caught us a troublemaking abolitionist," Corey says, putting his hand down.

The man with the rifle nods. "I appreciate that. But you don't want to hang a person without a fair trial, do you?"

"Trial! We don't need a trial! I caught this troublemaker bothering my daddy's slaves myself," Corey says.

"Maybe so. You can say that at the trial, then."

One of the men who came up with the rifleman edges his horse close to you and lifts the rope from around your neck.

"Listen, Sheriff—" Corey begins.

The sheriff! He can't let them hang you.

"I don't like the abolitionists any more than you do, Corey," the sheriff says. "They don't understand that we have to have slaves to work the crops. But lynching is against the law—"

"You can just turn around and pretend you don't see us," one of the men with Corey says.

"Yeah," another says, "we'll do it quick-like."

This doesn't sound good at all. The sheriff is arguing with Corey and his men, and he might lose; after all, there are five against four.

"Now, listen—"

"No, *you* listen!"

Nobody is looking at you. You kick the horse with your heels suddenly, and it leaps away. The motion startles the other horses and they move uneasily, confused.

You've got a good head start before anybody starts to chase you. You ride into a thicker patch of woods a few hundred yards away and jump from the horse into a pile of leaves and brush. The horse keeps going. After a few seconds, the other horses and their riders thunder by, chasing the horse. You have only a few seconds before they realize you've jumped off. You don't have time to think of a new place— it's the rope or jail, for sure! Go back in time, fast!

Jump back to 1843. Turn to page 12.

You are in Philadelphia in the winter of 1849. It looks different from modern towns. Most of the buildings are wood, though some are brick or stone. And the people are wearing funny-looking clothes. The men have on fur top hats that look like stovepipes, long coats with two tails hanging down, and old-fashioned shoes with buckles. The women wear shawls and wraps over long dresses that are puffed way out. Many of them wear bonnets tied under their chins.

You ask a man where the black people in town live.

"Black people? You mean Negroes? Follow the road until you see a railroad track. Just past there." You thank the man and begin walking.

You come to a sign that says, "See the famous house of Edgar Allan Poe, the poet, only 1 cent." According to the sign, the house is only a few blocks away, to your right. A penny doesn't seem like much money! Things are certainly cheaper than in your own time.

The buildings and houses are getting smaller and more run-down as you walk north. Now you see several black people—but you must remember to say Negro instead of black, since that seems to be what people say in this time.

"Hello," you say to a girl about your age.

"I'm looking for Harriet Tubman. Do you know her?"

The girl looks at you oddly. "My name is—ah—Sarah Mae . . . Jefferson," she says. "Come with me."

She leads you down a dark alley into some old buildings. Inside a storeroom, you hear a group of men and women talking.

"—gwine back to fetch out her sister," a man says.

"—hopes she don't get caught," a woman adds.

"—lots of spies for the masters around," another man says.

"They talkin' about Miz Tubman," Sarah Mae tells you.

Just then, somebody inside calls, "Who's that out there?"

You realize they mean you. What should you do? They might think you're a spy.

Sarah Mae is in front of you. She won't see you if you jump. Should you stay and talk to these people? Or should you jump back to Dorchester County and try to find Harriet's sister before Harriet arrives to free her?

 Stay in Philadelphia. Turn to page 15.

 Jump to Dorchester County. Turn to page 22.

You are in Dorchester County in the summer of 1843. It's terribly hot. The dirt road is so dusty that clouds of dust jump at every step you take. Sweat runs down your neck and back.

You see a man working on a small garden, pouring muddy water from a wooden bucket onto the plants.

"Do you know a Harriet Tubman?" you ask.

"Can't say as I do," he says. "And I reckon I know just about everybody around these parts."

You thank him and walk on. After talking to a couple of other people you are no better off. One man says he knows a John Tubman but nobody named Harriet.

You walk through the summer heat to John Tubman's shack, but he isn't in. A small child tells you he is out in the fields working. "Ain't no Harriet Tubman," the little girl tells you.

Why doesn't anybody know her?

As you are thinking about what to do, a boy runs past you, yelling. "Fever! Fever!" He stops and starts talking to you, very fast. The

docta' done said there's four people with bullneck fever—the diphtheria! Say they probably
gonna die! Everybody got to stay away!"

That doesn't sound good, you think. You
can't find anybody who knows Harriet, and
there's a dangerous disease around, too. You
are sure Harriet is here—but wait! Do you
have the right name? Now you remember!
Harriet was married in 1844; before that, she
would have had another name, her maiden
name! She won't be Mrs. Tubman yet!

The only thing is, you don't know what her
other name might be. You can't go around asking for somebody who might change her name
someday. That won't get you anywhere. And
there is this bullneck fever, too. You decide
this doesn't seem like a very good place to look.

And you realize something else: Harriet
wouldn't know anything about the Underground Railroad yet, since she hasn't escaped
or begun working on it!

**Jump ahead to Dorchester
County, 1849.
Turn to page 1.**

You decide to stay and talk to these people in Philadelphia because you don't know anything about Harriet's sister in Dorchester County.

A big man looks out through the open door at you. "What you want 'round here?" he asks.

You take a deep breath. "I—I'm looking for Harriet Tubman," you say.

"What for? You not a spy for the slavers, are you?"

"No, sir," you say.

He smiles, looks at Sarah Mae, then says, "Come on in, then."

You and Sarah Mae walk into the room. The man tells the others that you are looking for Harriet Tubman.

One of the men stands up. "My name is . . . Joshua," he says. "I'm going on a—trip south pretty soon. To collect my wife down in Maryland. We might run into Miz Tubman on the way there or back. You can come with me if you want."

 Go with Joshua. Turn to page 16.

 Stay in Philadelphia and wait for Harriet. Turn to page 5.

You nod at Joshua. "I'd like to go with you," you say. Joshua may be a conductor on the Underground Railroad; his "trip" south is to free his wife.

You spend the afternoon gathering supplies which Joshua loads into two backpacks. He gives you one and carries the other himself. You start your trip by hitching a ride with a farmer on his milk wagon.

You think about asking Joshua about the Underground Railroad but decide maybe you should wait until he feels like telling you about it. You don't want to appear to be some kind of snoop or spy.

The trip to Maryland takes almost two weeks, another good reason for not waiting for Harriet to return to Philadelphia. Since travel is so slow, you might have had to hang around for weeks or months, waiting for her.

Most nights, Joshua pulls the wagon off the road and you sleep on the ground under the wagon. A couple of times, you stay in barns and burrow into sweet-smelling piles of hay to keep warm. Joshua has plenty of dried beef and beans, and sometimes you eat vegetables Joshua buys from farmers. He doesn't say much, but he smiles a lot. You begin to like him.

Finally, you arrive at a church just outside a

little village. It is late afternoon. Joshua looks at you and smiles. "Reckon I can trust you," he says. "We gonna meet some passengers here later tonight."

Ah, you were right! Joshua is a conductor on the Underground Railroad!

It is almost midnight when a dozen people begin to come out of the darkness to gather near the church's graveyard. There are three men, two women, and seven children.

Joshua looks upset. "Where is Lee Ann?" he asks one of the men.

"Done gone," the man answers. "Miz Tubman took her a few days ago."

Joshua nods. "Good. She'll be safe, then."

Everyone seems nervous. Joshua tells you that slave owners want to capture runaway slaves, but if they think they might get away, they shoot—to kill.

"Harriet is a few days ahead of us," Joshua says. "Maybe we'll catch up to her on the way back."

"We'll head straight north for about fifty miles," Joshua says. "There's a farm there where we can get new supplies before we push on to Philadelphia." He smiles. "The Big Cross Farm, we calls it. There's a hill behind the house with a cross on top of it—mus' be a hundred feet tall, dat cross. You can see it for miles."

In the darkness, you hear one of the women slaves singing very softly, "Follow de drinkin' gourd, follow de drinkin' gourd."

"Let's move out," Joshua says.

You begin to walk. Around the group, the night air is cold and clear and the stars overhead shine like sparkling dust. Suddenly Joshua stops.

"What's the matter?" you whisper.

"I thought I heard something—"

Somebody yells. "Hold it, you slaves!" A gunshot explodes close by!

"Slavers! They've found us! Run!" Joshua yells. "Everybody split up—head for the farmhouse I told you about!"

People crash through the darkness close to you; voices scream for you to stop. Another gunshot *cracks* in the night air, and Joshua falls with a groan. You stop and bend over him.

"Go on!" he says. "It's only my leg, but I can't run!"

"Maybe I can carry you—" you begin, trying to drag Joshua. No good, he's too heavy for you.

"No," he says. "I'll be all right. They'd rather keep me alive than let me die—I'm not worth anything dead. But you can do something for me."

"Anything," you say, watching the dark blood run down Joshua's leg.

"Miz Tubman has rescued my wife, Lee Ann. My real name isn't Joshua, it's Thomas—Thomas Dean. Get word to her and my daughter—she calls herself Sarah Mae Jeffer-

son—that I'm captured. They'll know what to do."

Thomas Dean! You came to find out about him!

"Hurry, before they catch you! Otherwise my family won't know what happened to me. You've *got* to tell them!"

There is another shot; the bullet whizzes by your ear. "Go!" Thomas says. You turn and run as fast as you can until you are far away.

Everything finally seems quiet after an hour or so, but now what? You're alone—and lost. How will you find your way to the farmhouse? It's a long way off, and you don't even know which way to start walking.

Wait. The woman back at the church was singing a song about the drinking gourd. Yes. You remember something about that now. One of the stars in the drinking gourd—also called the Big Dipper—points either to the north or south.

Wait. You think you know. You look up and see the stars which form the constellation called the Big Dipper.

 You decide the Big Dipper points north. Turn to page 30.

 You decide it points south. Turn to page 27.

You're strapped to a tree in Dorchester and feeling nervous—but, yes, one of the things you brought was a knife! You manage to pull it from your pocket and open it. It takes a few minutes to saw through the thick rope, but you finally make it. You're free!

Now what? You still think it's a good idea to find Harriet's sister, since she'd be a good lead. But when Corey Simon gets back and finds you gone, he might look for you, maybe with a mob who wants to *hang* you. Unless you can find a good place to hide . . .

Suddenly you hear hoofbeats. Maybe it isn't Corey. Maybe it's somebody else. Sure. Out for a ride in the cold, to this part of the woods? Not likely.

If you can find some local abolitionists to help you, you might still find Harriet's sister. On the other hand, if Corey catches you, you will definitely be in big trouble. Maybe you should have stayed in Philadelphia instead of coming back here. After all, you don't know anything about Harriet's sister, not even her name!

Jump to Philadelphia, 1849. Turn to page 10.

It's still cold in Dorchester County when you arrive. It's also cloudy and gray, and it looks as if it might rain or snow.

Your first thought is to ask for Harriet's sister, but you decide this might not be too good an idea. You got into trouble like that once, and somebody might remember you. Especially that mean kid with the whip. You don't want to run into him again.

As you walk along the cold and lonely road, thinking about the best way to find Harriet's sister, you see somebody on a horse. You wave, thinking it might be okay to talk to somebody alone. You can always get away from *one* person.

But it's Corey Simon! He pulls his horse up and sneers at you. "So you came back, eh? You should have kept running, troublemaker!" Before you can move, he pulls a big pistol from his belt and points it at you.

He walks you toward town. You realize you might be able to jump, but you don't want to do it with Corey watching you. Maybe when you get to the jail you'll be alone long enough to jump away into another time; that must be where he's taking you, to jail.

Wrong. He takes you into the woods and ties you to a tree! "You'll keep here well enough," he says, "until I get back with help—and a noose.

"We don't approve of people messing with our slaves around here, and we hang anybody who might be helping them to escape, be they slaves or free people!" He rides away.

Uh-oh. This won't do at all. You've got to do something.

If only you had a knife—wait. Maybe you do. You manage to work your hands into your pocket.

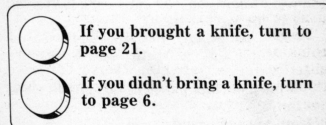

If you brought a knife, turn to page 21.

If you didn't bring a knife, turn to page 6.

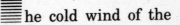he cold wind of the Philadelphia winter of 1849 chills you.

You shake your head at Sarah. "Sorry," you say. "I don't have any money I can use here."

"Well, that's all right. You can stay at my place. My aunt won't mind one more."

She leads you toward a really run-down section of town. It doesn't look much better than the slave quarters at Corey Simon's place.

Suddenly a heavy hand falls onto your shoulder. You turn and see a big, fat man glaring down at you.

"I don't know you," he says. "What are you doing in my part of town?"

"Just visiting, sir," you say. You wave at Sarah Mae. "I'm going to see my friend's house."

The fat man laughs. "Oh, ho! That's what you think!"

Sarah Mae whispers to you. "That's Fat Michael. He's the King of the Beggars! He has dozens of people begging for him on street corners. He takes all the money from them and gives them just enough to eat a little each day."

"What are you whispering about, girlie?" Fat Michael says.

"N—nothing," Sarah says.

Fat Michael looks at you. "You're a little too well-fed to be a proper beggar," he says, "but a few days of bread and water will fix that."

This won't do. Eating nothing but bread and water until you are skinny enough to pass for a poor beggar doesn't sound like fun at all. And if you're stuck on a corner somewhere, how will Harriet's friends find you?

You turn to walk away, but Fat Michael grabs you. "Where do you think *you're* going?"

"I—ah—have to—go to the bathroom," you say.

"The what? A bath? Baths are unhealthy! Look at me, I haven't had a bath for ten years!"

You noticed the smell; no wonder. "I mean, I have to go, I mean, to the—" You think fast. They didn't have bathrooms inside, you remember. "—To the *outhouse*, I mean!"

Fat Michael looks around. "There, there's a privy." He points at a small wooden shack.

Inside the privy, you look around. It is dark and smelly, and there is a loose board on one wall. If you jump, Fat Michael might think you managed to squeeze out through the board.

"Hurry up, it's cold out here!" Fat Michael says. "If you aren't out in thirty seconds, I'm coming in to drag you out!"

 Jump to Dorchester County. Turn to page 12.

ou're standing alone in the cold Maryland night, staring at the stars. You've remembered that the Big Dipper points in some direction, and you think it must be south. So, since you want to go north, all you have to do is walk in the opposite direction. You stumble along in the darkness looking for a warm spot to rest.

"Hey, there's one of them!" somebody yells. "The fool is heading south!"

Uh-oh. They've spotted you. You start running. So you should have gone *north*!

Suddenly you see five or six men in front of you. And there are at least that many more somewhere behind you. They are screaming to each other.

"Cut that way—block the path!"

"We've trapped this one, at least!"

You realize that they'll catch you if you don't do something. It's dark, and if you can jump, maybe they won't be able to see you. You'll have to take the chance.

"Where did—?" somebody says, and you know they've lost track of you for a second. Jump!

Turn to page 10.

ou pull the ten dollars from your pocket. In the cold Philadelphia winter of 1849, the money looks strange—it isn't even the same size as money in your time—but it's real in this time.

Sarah's eyes widen. "Where'd you get all that money? You rich?"

You shake your head. You remember the tour of Edgar Allan Poe's house was only a penny. "This is all I have," you say. "I'm not rich."

Sarah takes you to a rooming house. The rent for one week, including meals, is two dollars!

During the week that follows, you have plenty of time to explore the area you are in. For a quarter, you hire a horse-drawn carriage which takes you to the banks of the Delaware River, where you see three- and four-masted sailing ships. Not far away, you see the Liberty Bell, with the famous crack in the side. You visit the grave of Benjamin Franklin, the famous inventor and Revolutionary War hero. The city is full of neat old buildings: churches, theaters, restaurants. One night you eat steak, potatoes, and a giant salad, all for seventy-five cents, at a very nice restaurant. Philadelphia during this time is a very interesting place.

The only problem is that none of this is helping you to find Harriet Tubman.

Back in your room, you wonder what you should do. You know Harriet will be coming back to Philadelphia eventually—she lives here now—but you don't know when. You know that since she is traveling on foot, it might take a long time. Weeks, maybe even months!

Waiting in Philadelphia for Harriet wasn't such a hot idea: It won't take much of a time jump if you just go back a week or so and hop to Dorchester County, still in the winter of 1849.

 Turn to page 22.

Even though you're lost in a dark, cold Maryland night after being chased by slavers, you suddenly feel better. It might be the year 1849, but the stars haven't changed much from your own time. You look up and see the Big Dipper. It looks like a cup with a long handle. If you use the two stars on the outside of the cup as pointers, they'll show you the North Star, which will lead you north!

The next three days pass slowly. You must use the stars as your guide and travel at night, when you won't be seen. You manage to find barns to camp in during the daytime, burrowing deep into the hay to keep warm and hidden. You keep heading north, toward the farmhouse.

Finally, just at dawn, you find it. There is the giant cross on top of the hill, just as Joshua said. It's still a long way off, but this has to be the place.

You knock on the door, and a woman answers. After a few careful questions, you realize that this is the right house. You take a deep breath and ask if Harriet is around.

"She just left," she says. "Last night."

"Maybe I can catch her before she gets back to Philadelphia," you say.

" 'Tain't likely," she says. "She says she's got a couple of other stops to make. Might be a month or more 'fore she gets home."

Not too good, you think. You need to find her more than ever. Joshua—Thomas, that is—is wounded, and you must tell his wife. A month is too long to sit around waiting.

Hmm. You know Harriet was a nurse during the Civil War. Surely there would be records about her, telling where she was working? And perhaps those records would be in the War Office, in Washington, D.C.—that's where they were normally kept. You can jump forward in time, arrive in Washington during the war, and find the records on Harriet.

 Turn to page 36.

It's the fall of 1861, and the Union fleet has just blown the ferry you were riding on out of the water. You see a boat nearby and swim toward it.

"You all right?" a man with a thick southern accent asks as he pulls you from the water.

You nod.

"Them Yankees got us outnumbered," another man says. "We'd better hightail it out of here."

"I reckon you got that right," the first man says. He looks at you. "What do you think?"

You nod again. Better agree, otherwise they might think *you're* a Yankee—not a very good thing to be in this boat full of Confederates.

"They'll never catch us alive," another man says. Something about his voice sounds familiar. You glance at him. It seems as though you've seen him somewhere before. . . .

Oh, no! It's Corey Simon! He's older now, since this is years after you first met him, but it's Corey all right! Will he recognize you? You turn your head away and look out over the water as the little boat chugs toward the shore. Probably he won't remember you. After all, he wouldn't expect you to be the same age as when he first saw you. But what if he does? He's just mean enough to toss you back into the water!

As the boat reaches the shore, a party of men in blue uniforms suddenly appears. "Hold it, Rebs! You're our prisoners!"

You raise your hands along with the men in the boat. Captured! No way will they believe you aren't a rebel. If you even try to deny it, then you'll be in trouble with the real rebels. You can't win. You should have gone with the other boat.

You arrive on shore, near a thick patch of forest. As you are being marched through the woods, you surprise a deer, who jumps across the path. It startles the soldiers. One of the Union men shoots at it but misses. In the confusion, you and some of the men jump into the bushes and start to run.

"Halt!"

Another bullet whizzes by as somebody shoots again. Suddenly you trip and fall—and a man trips over *you*.

"You stupid fool!" a man shouts. "I ought to kick your head in!" It's Corey Simon. But there's another shot, and he jumps up and runs away.

Nobody can see you, you realize, so you figure it's time to get out of here. The other boat must be safer.

 Turn to page 34.

ou're floundering in the ocean near Hilton Head Island in the fall of 1861. You swim toward a rescue boat. A tall man leans over and pulls you from the water. "Are you all right?" he asks.

"Yes, sir," you say, looking around at the boat full of uniformed men. Blue uniforms, which means Union soldiers.

"Don't worry," the man says, "we'll have this battle won soon, and you can get back to your ship."

You realize he thinks you fell from one of the northern ships, and you don't think it would be a good idea to tell him differently. "Thank you, sir."

Well. You may be in the right place to find Harriet, but you're certainly in the wrong time.

The boat pulls ashore. You tell the man who helped you that you'll catch up with him in a minute—you need to do something first.

When he turns away, you slip behind a bush.

Jump to Beaufort, late 1862. Turn to page 40.

You are just outside the hospital in Beaufort and quickly find out that it's August 1865. The buildings look deserted and there aren't many people around. The war must be over.

You ask a man coming from the hospital about Harriet. "Not here," he says. "Most everybody has gone home."

Maybe you can find out from the records here where she went—then you'd still be on her trail!

There are still a few people in the hospital, so you wait until late at night, then slip inside and look for the record office. You find it quickly and use a candle to give you enough light to locate Harriet's records.

Aha. She's been transferred to a hospital in Fortress Monroe, Virginia. That's several hundred miles up the coast, at the mouth of the James River.

What now? Should you jump to Fortress Monroe and try to find her there? Or should you go back to 1862 and follow her up the river?

 Jump to Fortress Monroe. Turn to page 61.

 Jump to follow Harriet up the river. Turn to page 52.

ou are in Washington, D.C. It's winter again and chilly. There's a little boy standing on a street corner, selling newspapers. You notice that the papers are very thin, only a page or two, and they cost only a penny. The date on the front of the paper says January 3, 1863.

There are a lot of soldiers, dressed in blue uniforms, walking or riding horses through the dirt streets. While most of the buildings are wooden, like those in Philadelphia, there are some great marble structures. You walk past a huge post office, the Patent Building, and the Treasury Building before you see the Capitol of the United States. It looks funny, because the big white dome on top of the Capitol isn't there. They must be still working on it, since it's nothing more than a frame of steel girders covered with ladders and scaffolds.

You come to a bridge over a canal. As you cross the water, a horrible stink reaches your nose.

"Phew!" you say. You see a boy of about ten standing on the bridge. "What's that awful smell?" you ask him.

The boy points at the canal. You see some kind of dead animal floating by—it looks like a mule or a horse. Yuk! "Does it always stink like this?" you ask.

"Nope," the boy answers, "it gets really bad in the summer. People throw their dead animals into the water. And all the sewers empty into it, too."

You shake your head. You are glad you live in a cleaner time.

You notice a bunch of children on the other side of the bridge. They are laughing and talking. One of them smiles at you. "Did you hear about the proc—proclamation?"

You shake your head, and the girl points at a poster on a wall. It's titled The Emancipation Proclamation. It is a paper signed by President Abraham Lincoln, freeing all the slaves in the United States, and it's dated the day before yesterday.

You keep walking and come to a big building, the Armory Square Hospital. You ask a soldier there if he knows where the military records are kept, and he points to another building nearby.

You walk to the record hall. A clerk smiles down at you. "Yes?"

You take a deep breath. "I'm trying to find Harriet Tubman," you say. "She's a nurse. Her parents want to know where she is." That's probably true; if you were a parent, you'd want to know where your daughter was.

The clerk smiles and asks you to wait a moment.

You smile back. This will be easier than you thought.

Then the clerk comes back with a soldier, and you get a sinking feeling in your stomach.

"So, you're from Miz Tubman's parents, eh?" asks the soldier. He looks at the paper in his hand. "I guess it's all right to give you her address, then. She was assigned to Beaufort, near Hilton Head, South Carolina, in—" He stops suddenly. Casually, he says, "Where did you say Miz Tubman's parents are living these days?"

Uh-oh. You didn't say. You realize that this is some kind of test. If you give them the wrong answer, you might be in trouble. There's a war going on, and they might think you're a spy!

You take a deep breath. You remember Harriet's parents live either in Auburn, New York, or Springfield, Massachusetts.

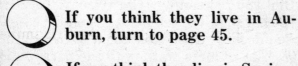

If you think they live in Auburn, turn to page 45.

If you think they live in Springfield, turn to page 60.

You are near Beaufort, South Carolina, outside a small bakery. You see a calendar in the window; it says the date is December 25, 1862.

The shop is closed, but there are a number of people walking around in the muddy streets.

Two Union soldiers walk by, talking. They are both black. "You goin' to the baseball game?" one asks.

"Yeah, I sure am," the other says. "It's New York style, with the hard ball, instead of that sissy Boston baseball."

Curious, you follow the men. You've never heard of New York or Boston style baseball.

You walk through the muddy streets and see that you're heading toward a bay. There is a large barge full of people at the end of a long wooden dock. A little steamboat is tied to the barge. The soldiers walk onto the barge, and you follow them.

"Looks like a good day for baseball out on Hilton Head Island," one of the soldiers says. "Me, I'm bettin' on the Forty-seventh New York Infantry to win."

"Nah," the other soldier says, "the Forty-eighth New York is gonna win this game, bet you a quarter."

You ask some people on the barge a few careful questions and find out that there's a "contraband" hospital at Beaufort. It sounds like the place you're looking for. But since it seems as if the whole town is going to this baseball game, you decide to wait until afterward to take the barge back; no point in losing the safety of the crowd. With all these people around, nobody will notice you.

The baseball field looks pretty much like the ones you are used to seeing in your own time. Only the men playing aren't wearing gloves.

While you are standing there watching, a boy walks over to you. "Do you know how to play baseball?" he asks.

You nod. "Yes."

He points at several other boys and girls nearby. "We want to get our own game going," he says. "Want to play?"

You think about that for a minute. You are waiting for the crowd to go back to town, anyway. "Sure," you say.

The bat looks funny—it's not much thicker than a mop handle—and the ball is also strange. It feels heavy, but it isn't the right size—it's sort of halfway between a hardball and a softball. And it looks as if it's wrapped in string. "Horsehair," the boy explains.

Your team is at bat first. Since you are new, they let you lead off. You stand at the plate—only a bare spot on the dirt—and position the bat over your shoulder.

The pitcher throws the ball. It comes straight at your head! You duck and the ball misses you. He's not a very good pitcher, you realize.

He throws the ball again, and it passes so far away you couldn't hit it if you threw the bat. Brother!

He winds up to pitch a third time. Just then a roar goes up from the crowd watching the soldiers play their game. Somebody must have hit a home run.

"Look out!" a girl screams.

You turn back to look at the pitcher just in time to see the greasy black ball coming straight at your head! You try to duck, but it's too late. The ball smacks into the side of your head, and everything goes black. . . .

 Turn to page 54.

You stare up at the soldier in the Washington record office. "Why, they live in Auburn, New York, sir," you say.

The soldier smiles and nods. "Of course. It says that right here—I should have seen it. Well, Harriet Tubman was assigned to Beaufort in 1862."

Aha! You're getting closer. There couldn't be that many hospitals in that area; she ought to be fairly easy to find.

It might be a good idea to check things out, though, instead of jumping right into the middle of something. After all, there's a war on, and a military hospital will have soldiers all around it.

You could jump into the area before the soldiers get there.

Or you could take your chances with the soldiers right now.

Hmm. What should you do?

 Jump back in time to Beaufort, 1861. Turn to page 46.

 Jump back two weeks to Beaufort. Turn to page 40.

You are in a clearing near Beaufort, South Carolina, in November 1861. The weather is cool, but a lot warmer than the winter you were in earlier. It should be fairly easy to wander around and find what you're looking for.

You come to the coast and see an island not far away. There is a small ferry—a steamboat with side wheel paddles—moored near the end of a dock. You walk out to it and see an old man, the operator.

"What is that island?" you ask.

"Hilton Head," the old man says.

Ah. According to the soldier, Harriet's hospital is somewhere close to Hilton Head.

"I wouldn't mind a passenger," the old man says. "I have to go out to pick up some freight. No charge 'cept your company."

You agree. Might as well as check things out.

As the little ferry chugs across the water, the old man points out Confederate soldiers and a big fort. "Fort Walker," he tells you. He spits into the water. "No way the Yankees will take that!"

You notice some smoke on the horizon. "What's that?"

He squints. "Looks like steamships," he says.

The ships come closer. The old man groans. "Oh, no! It's a battle fleet—of Union ships! We'd better make for shore!"

But the sea suddenly seems choppy and the little ferry can hardly move. Soon the Union armada is much closer. There must be sixty or seventy ships steaming and sailing toward you! As you watch, cannons begin firing from the fort at the ships.

The ships fire back. The air is suddenly filled with thunder! Cannonballs whistle through the air and explode in the water, shooting up big fountains of water.

Suddenly one of the ships turns toward the ferry. It's firing at you! The old man tries to turn the craft away, but the other vessel is much faster. The shells come closer and closer. Now they're spraying you with water!

Boom! The sky tilts, and you go flying into the air. The ferry has been hit!

You splash into the water, swallow a cold, salty mouthful, and bob to the surface. There's a big chunk of splintered wood floating nearby. You grab onto it.

All around you, the battle continues. Thick, greasy smoke floats over the water. The explosions of the cannons seem to go on without stopping, and whistling cannon balls land all

around you! There are pieces of ships, wood, cloth, and other debris floating all around in the water from ships which have been damaged by the fort's cannons.

You hear somebody calling. "Over here! Safety over here!" The voice is southern; it must be a rescue boat sent out to help the ferryman.

"Ahoy!" another voice calls.

The heavy smoke clears a little, and you see two boats. One group is wearing gray uniforms; the other group has on blue uniforms. Both seem to be looking for survivors in the water, and while you can see them both, they don't seem to see each other. You'd better try and paddle toward one of them. But which group?

 Choose the group in gray. Turn to page 32.

 Choose the group in blue. Turn to page 34.

he night you spend hiding on the Combahee River is very quiet. You shake your head. No matches! How are you going to steam away if you can't build a fire? And you can't use a plain dinghy. You'd never be able to row against the current for miles up the river.

Maybe one of those lamps, hanging near the end of the dock—maybe there are some matches there. You sneak carefully toward the light.

Yes, there are several loose wooden matches lying by the lamp. You pick them up and start back toward the boat.

There's a noise behind you! Is it the sentry? You crawl along the dock quietly.

Near the boat, you start to hurry. Just as you reach it, you trip and fall, dropping the matches and smacking into a thick piling with your head. Oh, it hurts! You feel dizzy for a few seconds.

Maybe you should forget this whole idea and jump back to the hospital. Your head is really throbbing. Or should you find the matches on the dock and keep going?

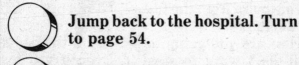

Jump back to the hospital. Turn to page 54.

Keep after Harriet. Turn to page 58.

ou find a farmer who is heading north and hitch a ride with him on his wagon. Finally you arrive at a dock on the Combahee River, close to where it empties into the Atlantic Ocean. There's a sentry standing by a line of small steam and rowboats moored to the dock.

"I have an important message for Colonel Montgomery from Dr. Durrant at the hospital," you say.

"Too bad," the soldier says, "you just missed them. They left two days ago, going up the river."

"Could I borrow a boat, then?" you ask.

The soldier scratches his head. "I'd have to check it with the sergeant," he says.

"Never mind," you say. If the sergeant checks with the hospital, he'll find out that you're not an official messenger of any kind. True, your mission is very important, but they might not understand—and you can't tell them you're from the future. They'd put you in an asylum.

How are you going to get one of the boats? You don't want to steal it. Even if you just borrowed it and then brought it back, they might not understand.

As you are walking away from the dock, you see something shiny in the dirt. You pick it up and look at it. It's a coin, and from the looks of it, made of gold. You rub the dust off and see that it is a Spanish gold piece!

The coin is tarnished and worn. It must have been lying there for years. Maybe it was even dropped by pirates. What luck! Just what you needed.

You hide until dark, then slip back onto the docks. You'll leave the coin on the dock as payment for the boat. Gold is pretty valuable, and things cost a lot less in this time. Probably they could buy a whole new boat for what the coin is worth, and anyway, you plan to bring it back once you find Harriet.

It isn't stealing. You're only renting the boat, and they have plenty of them to spare.

You choose the smallest and oldest of the boats, one with a tiny steam engine. You know you have to build a fire in the box under the boiler to start the steam working. It's dark and quiet, and you search your pockets for matches to start the fire.

 If you brought matches, turn to page 58.

 If you didn't bring matches, turn to page 51.

You open your eyes. A bearded man with a white apron spattered with brown is standing over you.

"Ah—awake, I see," the man says. "You must have taken a nasty crack on the head," he says, "judging from that lump."

You touch your head. Ow! There's a goose egg on your head, all right, and it's sore.

"Well, I think you'll be all right now. A little rest will fix you up." He turns and walks away. You look around. It's a hospital. You're lying in a bed, in a ward, with other beds and patients. Well, this wasn't how you'd planned to get here, but this must be the same hospital where Harriet works. You're getting closer!

The patient in the next bed moans. You look at him. He's a young man of about twenty, and he's mostly wrapped in bandages. "What happened to you?" you ask.

"Our mortar blew up," he says. "Set the whole camp on fire. I got burned."

You see that the bandages are stained red and yellow in places.

The man continues. "I'll be all right, though, thanks to Miz Tubman."

She's here! Before you can ask the man

about her, he says, "It's a good thing you woke up when you did—they were fixin' to put the leeches on you."

"Leeches? What are leeches?"

The man laughs. "They're sort of like slugs, with teeth. They stick 'em on you and let them suck the bad blood out."

Ugh! Slugs, with teeth? How awful! And they suck out your blood? You're glad you woke up.

"You know Harriet Tubman?"

"Sure. She's the best nurse in this place. Before the war she risked her life lots of times to free slaves. A fine lady."

You remember how dangerous it was on the Underground Railroad yourself. Yes, Mrs. Tubman is very brave. And now she is taking care of the sick and injured. "Listen," you begin, "I have to talk to Harriet Tubman. It's important. Which one of the nurses is she?"

There are six or seven women walking around the the big room, working on patients—sponging them with cool water and giving them medicines.

"Oh, none of them," the burned man says. "She's gone."

Gone? Oh, no. "Do you know where?"

"Sure. She went with Colonel Montgomery on his gunboat up the Combahee River. They're collecting more of the rebel torpedoes—that's a kind of floating mine—left to blow up our ships. The river is thick with them, so I hear. Some places they say you can almost walk across from shore to shore without getting your feet wet by stepping on the torpedoes. Harriet, she's there to talk to the slaves the colonel frees along the way. They trust her."

Your hopes fall like a rock dropped off a roof. She's not here! Sure, she's doing good work, risking her life again, but that doesn't help you at the moment. "Well," you say, "do you know when she might be back?"

"Can't say. Last time, they were gone two weeks, collecting torpedoes and freeing slaves. Could be that long this time, too. Maybe longer."

Oh, no. You don't want to wait weeks! Not when you feel Harriet is so close. Maybe you can find her. "Where is this Combahee River?" you ask. Can you get a boat?

"About fifteen miles northeast of here, I reckon."

Hmm. You can go after Harriet. Or you could jump ahead in time and hope to catch her here when she gets back—perhaps near the end of the war, when things are quieter.

 Go after Harriet. Turn to page 52.

 Jump ahead to a time late in the war. Turn to page 35.

n the darkness on the Combahee River dock, you search your pockets quickly, looking for—

Yes, you find the matches. They seem a little damp and feel kind of greasy, but you manage to get one lit. It flares brightly in the darkness. You cover it with your hands and light some dry kindling to start a small fire under the boiler. You keep adding wood until you have a hot fire going. The pressure in the boiler begins to build as the water inside boils.

"Hey! Who goes there?"

The sentry! And he sees you!

You hope there's enough steam built up to turn the paddle wheel on the little boat. You turn the control. . . . Yes!

You cast off the line holding the boat to the dock and begin to pull away into the swirling water. You remember to toss the Spanish gold piece onto the dock.

"Halt! Halt or I'll shoot!"

You duck down behind the boiler.

Blam! Ting! The bullet hits the steel plate close to your head. Your ears ring from the sound. "Halt!" the guard yells again.

You are almost in the middle of the wide river, a long way from the dock. It will take the guard a minute to reload his rifle. You smile in the darkness. If they want to chase you, it will take them some time to build up steam in another boat; besides, you left the coin.

Once you get a good way from the dock, you decide to slow down a little. The paddle wheel is churning the water pretty fast, and since it's dark, you don't want to bump into a sandbar or something.

The moon comes from behind a thin cloud, and you can see a little better. It's a nice night. Hmm. It looks as if there is a big log just up ahead. You turn the steering control of the boat, but it looks as if you are going to bump the metal-covered log anyway.

Metal-covered log? Logs don't have metal on them!

Suddenly you remember what the man in the hospital bed next to yours said about the river: It was full of Confederate torpedoes— mines which can blow up ships!

You dive into the icy cold water just before the boat smacks into the torpedo—

There is a BOOM! so loud your ears hurt. The little boat blows sky-high in a blast of orange flame. A giant wave heads toward you as pieces of the little boat rain down around you. The wave will probably drown you! No time to think. Jump!

Turn to page 46.

The soldier behind the clerk in the record office stares at you. You think Harriet Tubman's parents live in Springfield, Massachusetts—but what if they don't?

You decide to try to bluff the soldier. "Why, they live in the same place they've *been* living," you say.

The soldier looks at you more sharply. "And just where might that be?"

Uh-oh. He's called your bluff. You smile. "Springfield, Massachusetts, sir."

He shakes his head. "Wrong!"

You'd better do something, quick. "Look out, he's got a gun!" you scream, pointing at the wall behind the soldier.

Both the soldier and clerk spin around to look. You take off through the door as fast as you can.

You think you have a good lead, but the guy must be some kind of champion runner. He's gaining on you, fast!

Better find a place to hide and jump. You know where Harriet was assigned, but not when. Maybe if you go back in time to Beaufort, you can be sure of catching her.

Jump to Beaufort, South Carolina, in 1861. Turn to page 46.

You are near Fortress Monroe, Virginia, in August 1865. The fortress is right on the water, and there are ships anchored nearby. Things look quiet. The war must be over, all right. You relax a little. Maybe people won't think you're a spy and you can find Harriet and get on with your mission.

You see a boy about your age walking toward you. He is black and wearing a new pair of pants and a shirt, but no shoes. "Hi," you say.

"Hi to you, too!" he says.

"You sure seem happy."

"Oh, yes, I'm happy, all right. The Union men finally got around to 'mancipatin' me from my plantation. I'm going north to the free lands to make my fortune! I got me fifty cents. The first chance I get, I'm gonna buy me some new leather shoes with it!"

You smile back at him. Fifty cents for a pair of shoes. Back in your time, fifty cents would barely buy a pair of *shoelaces*!

The boy leaves, and you begin to walk across a wide field toward some buildings. But before

62

you get halfway across the field, the dark
clouds in the distance get closer. It looks like a
summer storm, coming in fast. You start to
run, but in a couple of minutes the rain is
coming down really hard. Then lightning
starts to flash and thunder booms.

You are really drenched now. Water is running down into your eyes, and your clothes feel
as if they weigh a hundred pounds. Your feet
sink into mud at every step.

There are some trees just ahead; maybe
they'll stop some of the rain and wind. You
slog toward them.

The lightning is getting closer, though.
You'd better hurry—

Flash—BOOM! You are knocked down! The
lightning has hit right next to you! As you roll
over and look up, glad that it missed you, you
see that it has hit a tree—which is falling
right at you!

You have to jump, quickly! The tree will
squash you like a bug if you don't get out of
here!

 **Jump back in time! Turn to
page 75.**

ou are in Baltimore in December, 1860. Brr. Another cold jump; this time, there is snow piled six inches deep on the ground. The city, like Philadelphia and Washington, looks very interesting, but you don't have time to enjoy it. You know you are getting closer to your goal when you find an old black man who tells you Harriet Tubman left only three days ago with a group of seven people, including a baby.

"They's a-headin' for freedom in York," he says, shaking his head.

"Why didn't you go with them?" you ask.

"I'se too old," he says. "And besides, my mistress is very kind to me."

You shake your head. No matter how kind your owner might be, you wouldn't want to be a slave.

This time, you plan to do things a little differently. You ask around and find out that the Railroad route curves off to the west, to a secret "station." You also find out how far people can walk in a day—only twelve to fifteen miles, usually—and decide you'll get *ahead* of them. You can jump, oh, say, fifty miles or so, to the north and west, find out who the local Underground Railroad people are, and be *waiting* for Harriet's group when they get there!

You jump. You find yourself in a wooded area by a little hill. A farmer working nearby tells you where you are: near a little village called Gettysburg, Pennsylvania.

You go into the little town and see a group of people in plain gray clothes coming out of a Quaker meetinghouse. Perhaps one of them will know about the Underground Railroad. As you draw near, you overhear a man speaking to a pleasant-looking woman.

"I've just received word, Mrs. Dodds, that a group of runaway slaves will rest on Cemetary Ridge tonight. Dost thou have any food for the poor people?"

"Aye, Mr. Phelps," she answered. "I believe I have some cold mutton and cornbread in the pantry. They're welcome to that and more."

You are pleased to discover that Harriet will be arriving tonight.

You find your way out to Cemetary Ridge and wait. The cold bites at your face and you have to keep walking around to keep warm, but it's worth it if Harriet gets here soon.

It is nearly morning when you see a group of people coming up the ridge. A big woman, dressed in a long dress and heavy coat, is leading them. It must be Harriet! Finally!

You hear a squeaky sound and hoofbeats, and from the other side of the ridge you see a wagon with two men in it. That must be the "conductors" with food for the refugees.

Slowly and carefully, you walk toward the slaves. There are only three women, you see when you get closer, and any of them could be Harriet. You were sure you'd spotted her, but now you aren't at all certain which one she is.

The three women separate themselves from the others and walk toward the conductors to get the food. You hear them talking.

"What you reckon they's bringin' us to eat, Rebecca?"

"I dunno, Sarah. Something good, I hopes. Think so, Moses?"

"I sure hopes so too; I'se getting real hungry."

One of the women sees you. "Who are you?" she asks, looking suspicious.

"A friend of—of Mr. Phelps," you say.

The one named Sarah smiles at you. "Well, we sure can use friends, all right."

The woman named Rebecca says, "I'm gonna go see to old Mr. Jenkins, he's ailin' with his bones. And my baby is hungry."

You are left standing next to Moses and Sarah. One of them must be Harriet. You start to ask when you hear dogs barking!

"Up this way!" a man yells. "I see 'em!"

Uh-oh. Slavers!

The two women next to you yell a warning

to the conductors, turn in different directions, and start to run. They must have a plan worked out for emergencies like this, you think. But you need only a minute or two to talk to Harriet to complete your mission!

You know Harriet won't get caught—she goes on to become a nurse for the Union, after all. But which one is she? You need to follow the right one!

Follow Sarah. Turn to page 92.

Follow Moses. Turn to page 94.

ou discover from a woman carrying a bucket of sour milk that you are near Port Royal, Virginia—but that it's April 25, instead of April 26, the way you'd planned. And it's almost dark, too. The meeting of the abolitionists won't be until tomorrow.

You see that you're on the edge of a farm. There are some short, leafy plants growing in the field. You aren't sure what they are until you get closer. They have a familiar smell.

Of course, you realize. They're young tobacco plants.

It is getting late, and you need a place to camp for the night. You see a farmhouse with trees around it, and beyond that, a big barn. You decide you can sneak in there and sleep in the warm hay. That won't bother anybody.

You are pretty tired, so you pick out a pile of thick, dry hay, burrow into it, and quickly fall asleep.

You awaken to the sound of shouting.

"Come out!" a man screams. "Surrender or die!"

You gulp and take a deep breath. Are they talking to you?

"Never!" another voice yells back. You suddenly realize you aren't alone in this big barn. Quietly you push aside the hay.

The inside of the barn is pretty dark, but you can just make out a man standing a few feet away. He is hobbling toward the door, using a crutch, and carrying a short rifle in the other hand.

There are more shouts from outside. You sneak from the hay, being as quiet as you can, and make your way to a crack in the outer wall.

Outside there are a lot of soldiers: at least twenty-five, some of them holding torches. As you watch, one of them rushes to a small door in the side of the barn and tosses a torch inside!

The dry hay quickly catches fire. Suddenly you can see things all too well: the man with the crutch and rifle is—is—John Wilkes Booth! The man who shot Lincoln!

As Booth moves toward the door of the barn, a shot booms out. Booth falls.

"Got him!" somebody yells.

Instantly the doors are rushed and shoved open, and Booth is dragged out by the heels. All the men seem to be watching him, so you run to the door and slip outside.

Some of the soldiers begin throwing water from buckets onto the fire, but it doesn't seem to help much.

You see the soldiers have dragged Booth to the porch of the farmhouse. It looks as if he's been shot in the head.

One of the soldiers sees you. "Hey!" he yells. "Who are you? What are you doing here?"

Uh-oh. These men are all pretty excited about capturing Booth. You doubt that you'll be able to explain who you are without raising their suspicions. "Look out behind you!" you holler.

The soldier turns.

You run back into the burning barn.

"Hey, stop!" another soldier yells.

Most of the barn is in flames now. Smoke gets into your eyes, and you choke and cough. Got to jump out of here, fast.

Where was it Harriet was going to be? Baltimore? 1860? And somewhere else? No time, the fire will get you!

**Jump ahead to Baltimore,
December 1860.
Turn to page 64.**

You awaken to the sound of drums. You look around and realize you are in a hammock inside a wooden warship.

You scramble up onto the main deck. Off in the distance a cloud of black smoke appears. "That's it!" somebody says. "That's the awful iron ship!"

You watch as the cloud gets closer. Soon you can see the ship. It's the same one you saw yesterday—the *Virginia*, the one that looked like a barn roof.

The *Minnesota* is still stuck on the sandbar. The *Virginia* gets closer and closer.

Suddenly, the little flat ship, the *Monitor*, heads straight at the oncoming monster. As it gets closer, a port opens in the tin-can-shaped turret—and a cannon barrel pokes out! The cannon fires a blast of fire and smoke. A cannonball smashes into the *Virginia*!

You and the men on the *Minnesota* cheer. Then you all grow quiet. The cannonball has bounced harmlessly from the thick iron plates of the *Virginia*.

Now the *Virginia* lets go with a full blast from what looks like four cannons. One of the balls smacks into the *Monitor* with a loud clank. It leaves a round dent, but otherwise the little ship looks okay. More cheers from the *Minnesota*.

For hours the iron ships circle each other,

firing black clouds of smoke from their cannons. Suddenly the bigger ship, the *Virginia*, tries to ram the *Monitor*!

The smaller ship pulls away just in time.

Then, while the *Monitor* is turning around, the big ironclad *Virginia* swings toward the *Minnesota*!

You hear Captain Van Brunt yell "Fire!"

A big gun goes off. The deck vibrates under your feet. A cannonball whistles past the *Virginia*. A miss!

The iron ship fires back at you. A hit! There is a terrific explosion, and flames leap out from under the deck. Men scramble to put the fire out.

The *Virginia* fires again. The shot sails past and hits a small tug which has been trying to free the ship. The tug explodes with a shower of wood and metal flying in all directions.

It looks bad. Maybe you should jump before the ironclad blows this ship to kingdom come! Another cannon shell booms from the *Virginia* toward the *Minnesota*. But in the water, you see the *Monitor* swinging around to attack the bigger ironclad. What should you do?

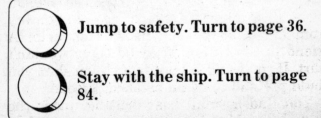

Jump to safety. Turn to page 36.

Stay with the ship. Turn to page 84.

ou are standing next to the same tree that was going to crush you; it shows no sign of being hit by lightning now, though.

You start walking. You see a man in a gray uniform.

"Please, sir, could you tell me the date?"

"Well, I reckon it's March the eighth, 1862," he says.

You thank him and move on. Hmm. You've jumped back just over three years. The war is still on.

From the bay come the sounds of battle. You see ships firing at each other. You look, but they are only blurs in the distance.

As it gets closer to evening, a strange-looking vessel steams in to a nearby dock. The ship looks almost like a barn roof, only it's covered with iron plates. You see that it's named the *Virginia*.

Well, this area is being held by the Confederacy, so it might be a good idea to get away from here. Maybe you need some help. A friend in the Union Army or Navy wouldn't hurt. If you could get out to a Union ship, you could pretend to be an escaped prisoner.

You find a small boat drifting under the dock. It has Union markings on it, so it must have broken loose from one of the Union ships during the battle. You'll return it to them.

After what seems like hours of hard rowing, you see several ships nearby. Even though it's dark, the ships have lanterns lit, and you can see the name of one of the warships: the *Minnesota*. You row toward her.

Suddenly a light glares in your face. It's a Confederate patrol boat, and they see you!

"Halt, or we'll shoot!"

You row frantically and manage to get out of the light. It will only be a few seconds before they spot you again.

You're close to the ship. You can probably make it. On the other hand, you could jump back to Washington, D.C., and find a library. By now Harriet has surely had stories written about her—the days of the Underground Railroad are years past.

"Hey, stop, y'all!" somebody on the rebel patrol boat yells at you. Then you hear the explosion of a revolver. The bullet splashes into the water far to your left.

They haven't spotted you yet. Better decide what you're going to do.

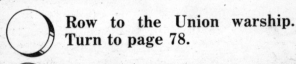

Row to the Union warship. Turn to page 78.

Jump to Washington, D.C. Turn to page 80.

ou row for all you're worth toward the Union warship. The lantern's glare finds you again. Another shot cracks the warm night air. Another miss! You hear men shouting from the warship *Minnesota,* then more shots, this time from the ship at the rebel patrol boat. The rebels are yelling.

"Let's get out of here!"

"Blasted Yankees!"

Safe!

"What happened?" a man asks you as you climb up a narrow ladder onto the wooden ship. "You escape from the Confederates?"

"Yes," you say. It's the truth.

You are introduced to Captain Van Brunt.

"Uh—" he says, looking as if he has something else on his mind, "I'll have to talk to you later, I'm afraid. I've got work to do."

A cabin boy comes over to you.

"Hi, I'm McCarthy. Welcome aboard— though it's not all that safe here, now. The ship is stuck on a sandbar," he says, shaking his head. "And we've got to get off by morning, or else."

"Or else what?"

"Or else that terrible iron ship will come back and get us! It sank the *Cumberland* and burned the *Congress* yesterday and almost got us, too. It's sure to come back and finish the job tomorrow!"

McCarthy takes you below decks and gets you some dried food, salt tack, to eat. Then he shows you to a spare hammock. You climb in and finally drift off to sleep.

Some time later, you wake up and hear people talking. It's still dark, but you go up on deck and see a ship pulled up next to you. What a funny-looking ship it is!

"Looks like a tin can on a shingle," you hear one crewman say to another. And so it does.

McCarthy, the cabin boy, scurries by. "What is that?" you ask, pointing at the strange ship.

"That's the *Monitor*," he says. "It's made of iron, like the one that attacked us yesterday. It's supposed to protect us from the *Virginia*—that's the killer ship from yesterday—but I don't know. I don't even see any guns on it! I think we're doomed!"

There's nothing you can do but get in the way up here, so you go back down to the hammock and eventually fall back asleep.

Turn to page 72.

ou are in Washington, D.C., in February 1863, just under a year since your encounter with the rebel patrol boat near the Union warships in Virginia. You figure that since Washington is the capital, it should have a big library with all the major magazines and newspapers of the day. If there is anything on Harriet Tubman or the Underground Railroad, it would be in a library.

While you are looking for the library, you go around a corner. A tall man bumps into you and nearly knocks you down. He curses and shoves you from the wooden sidewalk into the dirty street. "Out of my way!" he says.

You stand up and brush the dust off. How rude of him! As you look at the man, you realize that he seems familiar. Where have you seen him before?

Oh, no. It's—it's—Corey Simon! But what is he doing in Washington, dressed in regular clothes? You know he's a slaver. Surely he wouldn't have gone over to the Union cause. Maybe he's a spy!

You decide to follow him. It isn't likely he'll recognize you, especially if you stay far enough back.

After a block or so, Corey Simon walks into a shop. You peer through the window after him and see that the place is a kind of general store, selling all sorts of things. Since there are other people inside, you decide you could go in.

You see Corey Simon standing near one corner. Someone is standing next to him. You move closer, pretending to look at a rack of shovels and axes. There is another man talking to Corey, with short, dark hair and a thick mustache. You can hear them even though they're talking quietly.

"You have my information?" the man with the mustache asks.

"Yes," Cory says, pulling a paper from his pocket. As he does, something else falls from his pocket and clunks against the unpainted wooden floor. It bounces—right onto your foot!

What should you do? Ignore it? No, that would be suspicious. Quickly you bend and pick the thing up.

It's a gun, a small pistol! You just have time to notice it has the words "Deringer" and "Philadel" printed in the metal, between two engraved leaflike scrolls, just behind the hammer. Then Corey says, "Give me that!"

You hand it to him and quickly turn around so he won't get a good look at you. He might

not remember you from his plantation years
before, but he bumped into you in the street
only a few minutes ago. In fact, it might be a
good time to leave the store.

As you begin to walk away, you hear Mustache say, "Nice-looking little gun."

"You like it?" Corey says. "You can have it,
Mr. Booth. You may need it."

Outside, you think about Corey Simon. Obviously he's up to no good. But what should
you do? You do have a mission to accomplish.
Probably you can find a library now. When
you think about it, though, it might be better
to jump ahead in time to a point after the war
ended to look for articles on Harriet; that way,
you won't be thought a spy.

But Corey Simon might be up to something
nasty, and you're curious. What should you
do?

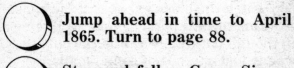

Jump ahead in time to April
1865. Turn to page 88.

Stay and follow Corey Simon.
Turn to page 86.

You're standing on the wooden deck of the Union warship *Minnesota*, aground on a sandbar at the mouth of the James River in Virginia in March 1862, being attacked by the *Virginia*!

The *Virginia* bears down on the *Minnesota* to fight the *Monitor* again. For another hour, the battle goes on—shooting, explosions, whistling cannonballs, black smoke as thick as heavy fog.

Then, suddenly, the *Virginia* turns and steams away!

You watch the black exhaust of the big ship as it heads toward port. It must be damaged, even though nothing shows on the outside. Or maybe it just ran out of cannonballs?

It doesn't matter. The *Monitor* didn't sink the *Virginia*, but it did fight it off and save the *Minnesota*! A little bit better than a tie, you think.

Tugs come up and begin pushing the *Minnesota*, trying to free it from the sandbar. You wander over to look at the fire, which is almost out. Men are pouring water on the flames.

Suddenly a sailor yells, "Watch it, there's a keg of gunpowder by the fire! It might explode!"

McCarthy starts to run. You call to him, "Will it blow up the ship?"

"No, but you don't want to be close to it if it goes!"

You turn to run—and the keg of powder explodes! A chunk of wood flies through the air and smacks into the side of your head, hard! Everything turns into a red blur.

You fall to the deck. Just as you are about to black out, you realize you need a doctor. But you are feeling faint, about to pass out in all the smoke and stink of the gunpowder.

You jump blindly. As you lose consciousness, the only thought in your mind is to get to a hospital, somewhere, sometime. . . .

 Turn to page 54.

ou wait outside the store until Corey Simon comes out. Then you start to follow him. He walks quickly. You almost have to run to keep up with him.

Suddenly you lose him! Where did he go? He was right across the street, on the high wooden sidewalk, just in front of a leather shop. Then he seemed to disappear!

You run across the street looking for him. Somebody grabs you. It's him—Corey Simon!

"What are you doing following me?" he says, squeezing your arms tightly. "I saw you in the store. Who are you?"

"Wait," you say. "I—I can explain. Don't hold on so tight."

He relaxes a little.

"You see, it's like this: HELP!" You scream for all you're worth. Corey tries to clamp his hand over your mouth, but you bite him, hard.

"Ow, ow, you rotten—!"

"Hey, what's this?" It's a soldier, walking by.

"He's a spy!" you yell.

Startled, Corey shoves you away from him and turns to run.

"Hold it!" the soldier yells, reaching for a pistol in his belt.

Corey keeps running.

"Stop or I'll shoot!"

Corey dodges to the left and right, but keeps going.

Blam! The soldier fires the pistol.

Corey grabs his leg and tumbles to the dirty street. He's hit! The soldier has wounded him in the leg! The uniformed man goes running toward Corey.

He'll have a tough time explaining his way out of this, you figure. And thinking about that, you decided it would be a good idea to be gone when the soldier comes back to ask you some questions.

You duck behind the leather shop. Jumping ahead in time to when the war was over seems like a better idea than this one of following Corey Simon.

 Jump to Washington, D.C., in 1865. Turn to page 88.

You're in Washington, D.C. A look at a penny newspaper tells you it's April 14, 1865. You wander down a dirt street. It looks as if *all* the streets in this town are made of dirt. It's kind of funny to see big marble buildings like the Capitol next to dirt roads. Finally you find a library. It's almost closing time, so you hurry inside. You ask the librarian if there are any articles on Harriet Tubman. She smiles and nods and hands you an old newspaper.

The article is a long one, and you won't have time to read it before the library closes. But the librarian tells you they have several copies of that paper and you can borrow one. You thank her and leave with the paper.

You wander around in the dusk for a while, looking for a place with enough light to read by. Finally you find a shop with a lantern hanging in the window, on Pennsylvania Avenue near Ninth. You perch on an old wooden pickle barrel under the window and start to read.

The article tells you all about Harriet's slave-running days, of how she freed hundreds of men, women, and children. There are dates and places. This will surely help you find her! You remember how terrifying it was to hide in the dark. What you did only once, she did many times. She was really a brave woman.

You look up suddenly as a man races by on a horse. He looks as if he's in a big hurry. There is enough light from the almost full moon and stars for you to get a good look at him. He is wearing a long coat and a hat, and he has a thick mustache.

The man looks familiar. You're sure you've seen him before. But before you can remember where, he rides by, the hooves of his horse like little thunderclaps in the night.

You go back to your reading.

After a while, several men, including some soldiers, come riding up. One of them says, "Hey, did you see a rider go by here?"

You nod.

"Which way did he go?"

You point down Pennsylvania Avenue, in the direction of the Capitol. "He went that way, sir."

"Let's go, men!"

You yell after them. "Why are you chasing him?"

"He's John Wilkes Booth, and he just shot the President!"

You watch the men ride away. Booth! Now you remember: the man with Corey Simon, here in Washington earlier! The man Corey Simon had given a gun to, in that store! *His* name was Booth. And he had a thick mustache. It must be the same man!

The man who assassinated Abraham Lincoln!

If you had only done something when you had the chance. But you realize it's too late to help now. Besides, you can't change history, even though you might stop something terrible from happening.

After you finish reading, you have an idea of several times when you might be able to find Harriet. In December 1860, she was taking a group of slaves from Baltimore, Maryland, to York, Pennsylvania; on April 28, 1859, she was in Troy, New York, involved in a riot to free Charles Nalle, a light-skinned slave. But there is more.

There is an announcement that on April 26, 1865, a group of abolitionists will hold a party in Port Royal, Virginia, to celebrate the end of the war.

That's only sixty miles or so away from here!

Even if Harriet is not at the party, there's a good chance somebody there might know her. Which way should you jump?

 Jump to Baltimore. Turn to page 64.

 Jump to Troy, New York. Turn to page 120.

 Jump to Port Royal, Virginia. Turn to page 69.

You run through the darkness near a place called Cemetary Ridge, in December 1860, chasing a woman you think is Harriet Tubman.

"Sarah!" you yell. "Wait!"

The woman doesn't slow down, but you put on a burst of speed and catch up to her. "I need to talk to you! Your real name is Harriet Tubman, isn't it?"

"No! And I can't talk now! Fool, we's being chased by slavers!"

"But—"

"Oh, where is that hiding place? Moses said it was this way!"

Moses. Whoops—now you remember. Moses is Harriet's nickname! You followed the wrong person!

Well, even so you know Harriet isn't going to desert her people. You can stay with Sarah and meet Harriet at the hiding place.

Suddenly a dog comes running out of nowhere and jumps at you. You dodge and jump. He misses you by inches, but you lose your footing and trip! You get up, but Sarah is out of sight. Then you hear the hoarse yells of the slavers. They'll be on you in a minute!

Turn to page 88.

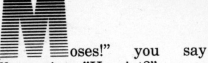oses!" you say breathlessly, still running. "Harriet?"

"Can't talk now," she says. "I got to get my people to the hiding place!"

It's Harriet! She runs to the group of people. "Get movin'!" she cries. "It's slavers."

One of the men moans. "Oh, no, they got us!"

Harriet grabs the man by the arm and jerks him to his feet. "They ain't got nobody yet. You get movin'!"

"I can't! I'm afraid!"

Harriet pulls a revolver from her coat and points it at the man. "Dead slaves tell no tales! You get movin' or I'll give you something to be really scared about!"

The man stares at the gun, then turns and starts running, fast. "Hurry!" Harriet says, waving the gun.

You all begin hustling along the ridge, away from the barking dogs and yelling slavers.

In the dark, you trip and roll down the side of the ridge. You hop up quickly, but the men and dogs are almost on top of you! You'll have to jump—you don't have time to run! Where? Back in time in this same spot!

Jump to Cemetary Ridge, July 2, 1863. Turn to page 99.

The mob around you is really getting ugly. People are pulling and shouting at the knot of men holding the man named Nalle. You manage to work your way to one side, to try and escape from the shoving crowd, but you are carried closer to the center of things before you can get clear.

You can see the sweat on the prisoner— you're pretty sweaty yourself by this time— and you see that his wrists are rubbed raw by the chains he's wearing. Two black women are pulling on Nalle's arms, trying to get him away from the white men. One of them lets go for a moment and stands there, looking almost as if she's asleep on her feet. The other woman is shoving one of the men holding the prisoner.

An elbow slams into the back of your neck, knocking you into a fat man's stomach. Oof! This is really dangerous. But you're sure Harriet Tubman is here. If you could see better through the crowd, you are sure you could recognize her. You know she helped Nalle get free. Probably she is one of the two women closest to him. But since you can't see them clearly, you don't know which one.

The woman who was pulling on Nalle the hardest is suddenly hit by one of the guards. She falls. The other woman, the one who seemed to be sleeping a moment ago, jumps back into the fight.

The first woman, the one who got knocked down, seemed to have been doing most of the fighting. Is it Harriet? Should you go and talk to her and let the mob move on? Or should you stay with Nalle, if you can?

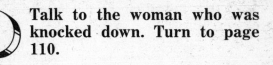

Talk to the woman who was knocked down. Turn to page 110.

Stay with Nalle. Turn to page 112.

Harriet is standing in the darkness of the graveyard, waiting for you to tell her if you're going with her to rescue Thomas Dean or not.

"I'll wait here," you say, "and stand watch."

"Fine. We'll come back for you—if everything goes all right." Abruptly she is gone.

You hear something in the bushes. Is that Harriet again? Did she forget something?

"Put your hands up or I'll shoot!" A tall man comes into sight. He has a shotgun pointed at your face. "Well, well. You abolitionists never learn, do you? We've been watching this church for years; every so often, we catch another stupid Yankee like you!"

You should have known that. You were here before! You should have gone with Harriet! She was your mission. How could you have let her out of your sight?

You start to back up. "Take it easy," you say. "I'm not what you think I am—"

You trip and fall into an open grave!

The man shouts and leaps toward you as you fall. But you are out of his sight for a moment. Jump away. There's no time to think where or when!

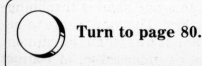

Turn to page 80.

You are on Cemetary
Ridge on the afternoon of July 2, 1863—just in
time to be knocked flat by a running man!
What—?

There is a terrible battle raging! All around
you, soldiers in blue are firing rifles. Cannons
boom and shot whistles past you. You shake
your head and stand up, only to be bumped by
another running man! Ouch! You feel dizzy.

Lying on the ground—where it seems safer—you can make out a little clump of trees
nearby. You hear men screaming; you see men
covered with blood sprawled all over the
ground. There are even dead horses at the bot-
tom of the ridge!

You crawl past soldiers, toward the grove of
trees. You make it just as a cannon shell whistles down a few feet away. The force of the
explosion lifts you into the air, and you pass
out. . . .

When you awaken, your head is throbbing
and your mouth is dry. The sun seems to be
higher in the sky than it was when the cannon
shell blew up. That's impossible, of course

. . . no, not if a whole day has passed. It must be July 3. You've been knocked out all night!

"Yeehaw!" A loud scream echoes up the ridge.

"Here they come, boys!"

You look down the ridge. Men in gray are charging up at you, rifles blazing, screaming like maniacs! You crouch down behind the tree while the men in blue and gray shoot at each other.

So many guns are going off that the smoke covers the ground like a thick fog. The wind shifts, and you see a group of gray-uniformed men still charging up the ridge. One of them has a flag—the Confederate stars and bars—and another is waving his hat on the end of a long pole. Shots keep blasting into the men, and they keep falling, red blotches staining their uniforms. This is horrible—all those people are dying, and they're all Americans!

The screams, the guns, the blare of bugles and roll of snare drums fill your ears.

Suddenly the last of the charging men is shot down. Things are deathly quiet.

You hear a man moaning just down the ridge. You work your way down to him. He's wearing a gray uniform, and he's been shot in the leg.

There's a part of a torn flag on the ground near the man. You quickly make it into a bandage and press it over the man's wound.

"Th-thank you," he says. He squeezes his

eyes shut for a minute, then opens them.

There's not much you can do. "I'll get a doctor," you say.

"It's all right. It doesn't hurt too bad. I reckon somebody'll get around to me, sooner or later. There's boys hurt a lot worse need the doctor more'n me." He looks at you. "My name's Private John Dooley," he says. "What's yours?"

You tell him.

"You don't look as though you ought to be here," he says. "But then, I guess none of us really ought to be here."

You nod. At least he's alive. A lot of men scattered up and down the ridge aren't.

Behind you, somebody says, "Dirty Yankee!"

You turn. There's a rebel sergeant lying on his side with his carbine leveled at you. He thinks you're an enemy! No time to explain to him—jump before he shoots! But where? You can hop a few months ahead and stay here; or maybe you can jump to Washington, D.C., again, two years from now, and check the library. But do it now!

 Jump a few months ahead to November 1863. Turn to page 104.

 Jump to Washington, D.C., 1865. Turn to page 88.

ou turn away from the ax buried in the stump and return to where Harriet Tubman and Lee Ann and Sarah Mae are hidden.

"Hey!" somebody says. A pair of strong hands clamp onto you. "What have we here?"

Oh, no! You can see a pale face in the dark.

You kick out, hard, and catch the man on the lower leg.

"Ouch! You rotten—!"

You twist away from his grip and run—away from where Harriet and the Deans are. If you'd been a few seconds slower, you'd have missed this man! Now you have to lead him away from Harriet and the others!

The man follows you in the night, yelling. You hope Harriet can hear him.

As you are running, you suddenly remember something important: According to the Data Bank, Thomas Dean *was* freed by four people with an ax! If you had taken the ax back to the other three waiting for you, you wouldn't have changed history. That's the way it really happened!

Too late now. The man behind you is gaining. But he can't see you. You'd better jump!

 Turn to page 112.

ou are on Cemetary Ridge. It's November 19, 1863.

The air is cooler and the smoke is gone. The battlefield is quiet, but blown-up cannons, broken wagon wheels, and rusty rifles are everywhere, along with blue and gray caps and hats.

You are tired, and you decide to find a place to eat and clean up. You walk along the ridge, heading for Gettysburg. Along the way, you see other reminders of the battle: torn-down tents, burned wagons, even a few worn boots. You imagine you can still smell smoke, even though you know it's been months since the Battle of Gettysburg.

In town, you find that a national cemetery is being dedicated today. A free lunch is going to be served, and the President of the United States, Abraham Lincoln himself, is going to be there. So you decide to go.

You follow the crowd. There are a lot of people: men wearing tall silk top hats and women in full dresses with lots of petticoats. You manage to find some fruit and slices of meat on a table, along with some bread. You take some of the food and munch it while walking around a big platform. Men with dark coats and trousers and top hats are seated on the platform. Suddenly one of them stands up. His face looks just like the head on a penny. It's Abraham Lincoln! He starts to talk.

"Fourscore and seven years ago our fathers brought forth on this continent a new nation, conceived in Liberty, and dedicated to the proposition that all men are created equal."

You worm your way toward the front of the crowd to see and hear better. People are murmuring as you squeeze between them.

"Now we are engaged in a great civil war," Mr. Lincoln says, "testing whether that nation or any nation so conceived and so dedicated can long endure. We are met on a great battlefield of that war . . ."

He keeps talking about brave men and the war and the great task before the country. The words are somewhat strange, different from speech in the future—your time—but you understand what he's talking about. He is sad about the war; he is sorry about the men who have been killed. The whole country must work together or it won't survive.

Suddenly you realize that this is the famous Gettysburg Address, which is engraved on the wall of the Lincoln Memorial in Washington, D.C., back in your own time.

Mr. Lincoln glances down at a slip of paper

and continues to speak. You notice that the paper looks like an old envelope.

Then, quite suddenly, he is through. Such a short speech! Politicians in your time might have talked for hours—Lincoln has only talked for a very few minutes.

Abraham Lincoln is a great man. You know the country will survive, but even Mr. Lincoln doesn't know that for sure at this time. His words are full of hope, though, and you wish you could tell him that the war will be over in less than two years, that this battle has been a major turning point.

But you're not allowed to change history. Your mission lies elsewhere. You need to go back and look up some information to get to where you need to be.

 Turn to page 88.

You and Harriet travel by wagon from Troy, New York, to Philadelphia in the spring of 1859. The trip lets you see the fresh greenery and flowers awakened from their winter's sleep. How sad, you think, that a great civil war is about to begin in a few years, a war which will kill thousands of people.

In Philadelphia, Harriet introduces you to Lee Ann Dean. You tell her your story.

"Alive? My Thomas is alive? Oh, Lord, thank you!"

A young woman, about ten years older than you, comes into the room. She looks familiar, and in a moment, you know who she is: Sarah Mae Dean—the girl you knew as Sarah Mae Jefferson. She's Thomas and Lee Ann Dean's daughter.

Sarah Mae is delighted by the news. She looks at you and smiles. "You look familiar, somehow," she says. "As though you were somebody I used to know a long time ago."

You smile at her but say nothing. They wouldn't understand about time travel, even if you could tell them.

The women sit down and make plans for the rescue of Thomas Dean. They will go into the slave territory and find out from their contacts in the area where Thomas was captured and where he is now. Then they'll sneak up at night and free him.

It seems like a simple plan. But you wonder about something: Thomas didn't seem like the kind of man to just sit around as a slave after he was caught. Why hasn't he escaped before now? Could the wound have been worse than he thought? What if he *is* dead?

Well, you'll have to find out.

 Turn to page 122.

You help the black woman who was knocked down by the guard to her feet.

"Are you all right?" you ask.

"I 'spect so," she says.

The mob has moved a block or so down.

"Are you Harriet Tubman?" you ask.

"Me? Laws no! My name is Catawba Jackson."

You sigh. Wrong again.

You hurry after the mob, but when you round the corner, they seem to be breaking up.

"What happened?" you ask one man.

"Nalle got plumb clean away!" he says, grinning. "Some woman pulled him loose and took off with him!"

Oh, no! "Which way did they go?"

"Got me. Got everybody else, too, looks like. Ain't that grand?"

Not from where you stand. You've lost her, just when when you were on the trail!

You're standing in the middle of the road, feeling miserable, when a group of men who are arguing come quickly down the street.

They aren't paying any attention to you, and by the time you look up, one of them walks right into you and knocks you down.

You try to roll out of the way, but one of the men trips and almost falls onto you. He jumps, to try and miss you, but his boot connects with your ribs—hard!

This was a mistake. You should have followed the other woman! In all the confusion, they won't see you if you just disappear. Jump back in time an hour or so and try this again!

 Turn to page 120.

The mob in Troy, New York, is pushing and shoving, but the woman who fell jumps back up and slugs the guard who shoved her down. You know the other woman is Harriet, though, because you remember that she has spells, caused by an injury as a child, so that she sometimes appears to be asleep or in a trance.

You follow the mob, trying to catch up to the woman. The shouting is louder and the men holding the slave Nalle are being shoved aside. Suddenly Nalle breaks away! Two people are pulling on him, a man and a woman. You are able to worm your way through the edges of the mob and follow them.

They take Nalle to a boat at the end of Dock Street and help him climb in. Then the men waiting in the boat row it across the river. People must have been ready to get Nalle away.

Now is your chance. You approach the short black woman. "Harriet Tubman?"

She looks at you. "That's me."

At last! You take a deep breath. "I'd like to talk to you, if I may."

She nods. "Sure. But come on, we don't want to stay 'round here; I reckon the law ain't gonna take too kindly to us freeing Mr. Charles Nalle!"

She leads you down a narrow alleyway between two wooden buildings, then on to a short street.

"Some friends of mine live down this way," she says.

You come to a small house, set back from the dirt road. Harriet leads you inside.

Finally you have a chance to look carefully at her. She isn't very tall, only about five feet or so, and she has a kind but strong-looking face. There is a scar on her head. That must be from her childhood injury.

Harriet introduces you to a man and woman in the little house, and the woman offers to fix everybody some tea. While she is gone, Harriet asks, "Now, what was it you needed to talk to me 'bout?"

You have a dozen questions, but the first one that pops into your mind is about the scar on her head. "How'd you get that," you ask, "if it's not too personal a question?"

She laughs. "No, I don't mind. When I was young, my owner, Master Brodas, he had a mean overseer who ran the slaves. One day, a boy decided he would take off from work and rest up a bit. The overseer, he saw him and began to chase him with a bullwhip. I chased after him to try to get the overseer to let him

be. That overseer, he picked up a scale weight, 'bout two or three pounds, I reckon, and threw it at the boy. Reckon I got in the way—that weight smacked me plumb in the head."

The woman returns with the tea.

Harriet looks at you and smiles.

"You come lookin' for me to ask me that?"

You shake your head. "No, ma'am. There are some—ah—stories told about the Underground Railroad and during the—" You stop. You were about to say "during the war," and since the Civil War hasn't started yet, you can't tell Harriet about it. Instead, you say, "during the time around now."

"What you want to know that for?"

"Not to get you into any trouble," you say. "It's very important."

She nods. "I'm pretty good at judging people," she says. "I reckon I can trust you. What do you want to know?"

"First, do you know a man named Thomas Dean?"

Harriet smiles. "Sure. Only his name is different on the Underground Railroad. He calls himself Joshua."

"Joshua," you say. "I mean, Thomas."

"Yes. He disappeared on a trip back to fetch out his wife Lee Ann. We figure he must have got killed."

"But he didn't!" you say. "I—"

You stop again. Better be careful how you say this: ten years ago, you would have been a lot younger—maybe too young to be traveling with Thomas on the Underground Railroad. "I . . . know about that trip," you say. "Thomas was only wounded in the leg."

"The slavers got him alive?"

"Yes."

Harriet smiles. "Lee Ann is sure goin' to be glad to hear that! And their daughter, she's grown and married now—she will be tickled to find her daddy is alive!" Harriet nods to herself, then says, "I reckon we'll have to go back and fetch out Thomas, now that we know where he is."

You smile at her.

She smiles back. "You been a big help to me. Ask me your questions."

You take a deep breath. At last! Your mission is about to be finished—

There is a knock on the door which quickly turns into a hard pounding.

"Open up! Sheriff's officers!"

"Quick, out the back way!" the man across from you says.

You and Harriet jump up and run to the back door. There is a tall wooden fence around the backyard; somebody is hammering on the gate to get in there, too.

"Over the top!" Harriet points at the back corner of the fence.

You obey. As you are climbing over the fence, you hear the woman who made you tea say, "Good luck, Moses!"

Harriet must be part jackrabbit, you think, as you watch her hop the fence.

A man comes around the corner. "There they are!"

"Come on!" Harriet says. "They could make a lot of money if they catches me!"

You run. You could jump away at any time, but you won't, not this close to completing your mission!

After dodging through several alleys, you manage to lose the men chasing you. You take deep breaths of air while Harriet grins at you. "You reckon you can tell me just where the slavers caught Thomas Dean?" she asks.

You think about it for a few seconds. You remember the place, but you aren't sure if you could tell her exactly how to get there. Still, you're sure you'd know it again if you saw it.

You tell Harriet this.

She nods. "Well, I can't ask you to go with us into that territory. It's pretty dangerous. What was it you wanted to ask me?"

You shake your head. This is what you came to find out. You can go and see it for yourself!

Turn to page 108.

You push away from the gravestone in the small churchyard and nod at Harriet Tubman.

"I'll go with you to rescue Thomas," you say. You haven't gone through all the adventures you've had to take a chance on losing contact now. You are almost finished with your mission: letting her out of your sight any longer than you have to wouldn't be very bright.

Lee Ann and Sarah Mae Dean are hidden behind a pecan tree, watching a run-down shack. "He's in there," Lea Ann whispers as you and Harriet walk up to the tree. "I saw him walk in front of the window!"

"Yes," Sarah Mae says, "but he's walking funny."

"He was shot in the leg," you say.

"Maybe, but that doesn't seem like it would make him walk the way he was walking."

Carefully, the four of you sneak toward the cabin. You dart ahead to peep into the window. Yes, it's Thomas. And he's alone. And you can also see why he is walking so oddly—he's chained to the wall with a thick metal chain!

No wonder he hasn't escaped in all these years.

Quickly you tell the others.

"There's an ax in a stump a little ways back there," Harriet says. She looks at you. "Run fetch the ax. The three of us will stay here and watch 'til you get back."

You nod and turn to run and find the ax.

Ah, yes, you see its handle there, just behind that pile of wood. . . . Wait. You stand alone in the darkness, staring at the ax. Can you do this? You aren't supposed to change history! If you bring the ax back to Harriet, will that change the way things happened?

What should you do?

Go back and tell Harriet you couldn't find the ax. Turn to page 103.

Fetch the ax. Turn to page 123.

Troy, New York, April 27, 1859. The afternoon air is cool but not cold, and you find yourself in the middle of a mob of shouting and shoving people. You see a sign that says you're near the corner of State and First Streets.

"What's going on?" you ask a man next to you.

He points at a second-floor window in a building across the street. "They got Charles Nalle up there in Mr. Beach's office."

You look at the window. There's a light-skinned black man framed in the window, looking out at the crowd.

A black man near you shouts at the crowd. "My name is William Henry! That's my friend they got up there. They say he's a slave in Virginia and they are goin' to take him back! It ain't right! He's been livin' as a free man!"

The crowd murmurs angrily in agreement.

"Yeah!"

"Right!"

"It's not fair!"

"Look! Here they come!"

The door to the building opens, and Charles Nalle is led out by several other men. His hands are chained together.

The crowd roars and pushes toward the prisoner. Three people reach Nalle at the same time—two black women and a white man.

Everywhere around you, people are cursing and shouting. Suddenly you get knocked down. This mob is dangerous! Maybe you'd better get out of here.

You get up. Should you stay and maybe be trampled by this mob? Or try another direction?

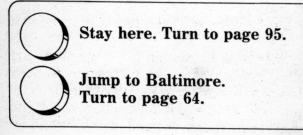

Stay here. Turn to page 95.

Jump to Baltimore.
Turn to page 64.

You are leaning against a tombstone in a little graveyard outside a church in Maryland. You have been here before, almost ten years ago, in 1849, when you met a group of slaves who wanted to escape to freedom. You are only a few days older, but ten years has faded the church and weathered the gravestones.

"Psst!" You hear a whisper and jerk around. "Everything okay here?"

You relax. It's Harriet. "Yes," you whisper back. "Did you find out where Thomas is?"

"Yes. At the Jasper Plantation. Lee Ann and Sarah Mae are watching the slave quarters now, waitin' for some sight of him."

He *is* alive. Good. "What now?"

"I'm going back there. You want to go or stay here?"

You think about that for a minute. What should you do?

 Stay and wait here. Turn to page 98.

 Go with Harriet. Turn to page 118.

You smile into the night as you stare at the ax in front of you. You were worried about changing time, but you've suddenly remembered that it will be okay to take the ax back to help Harriet and the Deans free Thomas Dean from his shackles in the plantation slave house. Because, according to the Data Bank, Thomas Dean was freed by *four* people using an ax! You'll be a part of history, but you won't change it!

Quickly you pry the ax from the damp wood. The metal makes a *skrinch* sound as it comes free.

As you are hurrying back toward the others, you see somebody walk by on his way to the main plantation house. Whew, that was close. If you'd been a few seconds earlier, you'd have bumped right into him!

Back at the slave house, you wave the ax. "Here it is," you whisper.

"Good," Harriet says. "Give it here."

She takes the ax and shoves the door open.

By the light of two candles, you can see Thomas Dean leap up. "Who's there—?" Then he sees Lee Ann, his wife.

"You came for me!" Thomas says.

"Sure," Lee Ann says, grinning. "Just took us a while, that's all."

"Stand back," Harriet orders. She whips the ax up and brings it down hard. Sparks fly

where the sharp blade meets the iron chain, but the chain holds. Harriet raises the ax again.

"I think I hear somebody coming," Sarah Mae says.

Harriet nods and whacks the chain again hard. It still doesn't break.

Voices come out of the darkness.

"Hurry!" Lee Ann says.

Harriet takes a deep breath and swings the ax a third time. Metal clashes against metal and—the chain parts!

Thomas Dean is free.

"Let's get out of here!" Harriet says.

"Well," Harriet says later, "you were gonna ask me something?"

You smile and shake your head. "No, ma'am," you say. "I don't need to anymore."

And you don't. By helping Harriet rescue Thomas Dean, you have learned the answer to your question. The diary was right; you were there to see it for yourself. You've accomplished your mission. "I'll be going now," you say, and you walk away from the group. When they are out of sight, you smile. Time to go home.

MISSION COMPLETED.

DATA FILE

Page 4: Harriet didn't marry John Tubman until 1844.

Page 11: What is Harriet's sister's name?

Page 15: Do you know when Harriet is coming back?

Page 20: A trip to the bank might help.

Page 45: Some places are safer than others; your timeline knows.

Page 50: Who is winning this battle?

Page 53: What did the wounded soldier say on page 56? Don't be thick-headed here.

Page 57: One, two, and three are good numbers, but what about the number four?

Page 68: Your Data Bank can help you here—if you know who Clark Kent is.

Page 91: Look at the dates and be exact—what do you know for sure?

Page 102: Where are you going? Your timeline knows.

Page 122: What is your mission?

About the Contributors

STEVE PERRY is the author of *The Tularemia Gambit* and the forthcoming *Hellstar* with Michael Reaves. His short fiction has appeared in various magazines and anthologies including *Galaxy, Asimov's, Fantasy and Science Fiction* and *Omni.* He is also co-author of Time Machine #3, *Sword of the Samurai.* He lives in Beaverton, Oregon, with his family.

ALEX NINO is an internationally respected illustrator. His work has appeared in such publications as *Metal Hurlant* in France, *Starlog* in America, and hundreds of magazines in his native Philippines. He is the illustrator of Time Machine #2, *Search for Dinosaurs,* and co-illustrator with John Pierard of Time Machine #4, *Sail with Pirates.* He is also the winner of an Inkpot Award.